The Princess
and the Pea

First published in 2005 by
Franklin Watts
96 Leonard Street
London
EC2A 4XD

Franklin Watts Australia
Level 17/207 Kent Street
Sydney
NSW 2000

Text © Anne Adeney 2005
Illustration © Gwyneth Williamson 2005

A CIP catalogue record for this book is available
from the British Library.

ISBN 0 7496 6157 7 (hbk)
ISBN 0 7496 6169 0 (pbk)

Series Editor: Jackie Hamley
Series Advisor: Dr Barrie Wade
Series Designer: Peter Scoulding

Printed in China

The Princess and the Pea

Retold by Anne Adeney

Illustrated by Gwyneth Williamson

FRANKLIN WATTS
LONDON•SYDNEY

Once upon a time there
was a royal family.

"Prince Hans needs a wife," said the Queen.

"But she must be a REAL princess!"

Lots of girls came to the palace.

Royal Notice:
Prince Hans is looking for a wife
Only real Princesses please.
STRICTLY NO servants or peasants.

Posh Pongy

Crowns -all sizes-

robe hire

Posh frocks

They *looked* like real princesses.

They *danced* like real
princesses.

They *smelt* like real
princesses.

But the King and Queen shook their heads.

They knew that none of them were REAL princesses.

One night, there was a big storm.

A wet, dirty and smelly girl knocked at the palace door.

"Please let me stay!" she begged. "I'm Princess Saffi." "Really?" said the Queen.

The girl did not look or smell like a princess.

"I will test her," said
the Queen.

"A REAL princess will feel this pea in her bed," said the Queen.

Then she told her servants
to put twenty mattresses
on top of the pea.

"You can sleep here,"
said the Queen.

Saffi climbed up to bed.

Next morning, the
Queen asked:
"Did you sleep well?"

24

"No!" said Saffi,
"I had no sleep at all!"

"It felt as if I was lying on a small bump," said Saffi.

She had felt the pea
through twenty mattresses!

Only a REAL princess
could have such soft skin.

So Prince Hans married
Princess Saffi.

And they lived happily
ever after.

Leapfrog has been specially designed to fit the requirements of the National Literacy Strategy. It offers real books for beginning readers by top authors and illustrators.

There are 37 Leapfrog stories to choose from:

The Bossy Cockerel
ISBN 0 7496 3828 1

Bill's Baggy Trousers
ISBN 0 7496 3829 X

Mr Spotty's Potty
ISBN 0 7496 3831 1

Little Joe's Big Race
ISBN 0 7496 3832 X

The Little Star
ISBN 0 7496 3833 8

The Cheeky Monkey
ISBN 0 7496 3830 3

Selfish Sophie
ISBN 0 7496 4385 4

Recycled!
ISBN 0 7496 4388 9

Felix on the Move
ISBN 0 7496 4387 0

Pippa and Poppa
ISBN 0 7496 4386 2

Jack's Party
ISBN 0 7496 4389 7

The Best Snowman
ISBN 0 7496 4390 0

Eight Enormous Elephants
ISBN 0 7496 4634 9

Mary and the Fairy
ISBN 0 7496 4633 0

The Crying Princess
ISBN 0 7496 4632 2

Jasper and Jess
ISBN 0 7496 4081 2

The Lazy Scarecrow
ISBN 0 7496 4082 0

The Naughty Puppy
ISBN 0 7496 4383 8

Freddie's Fears
ISBN 0 7496 4382 X

Cinderella
ISBN 0 7496 4228 9

The Three Little Pigs
ISBN 0 7496 4227 0

Jack and the Beanstalk
ISBN 0 7496 4229 7

The Three Billy Goats Gruff
ISBN 0 7496 4226 2

Goldilocks and the Three Bears
ISBN 0 7496 4225 4

Little Red Riding Hood
ISBN 0 7496 4224 6

Rapunzel
ISBN 0 7496 6147 X*
ISBN 0 7496 6159 3

Snow White
ISBN 0 7496 6149 6*
ISBN 0 7496 6161 5

The Emperor's New Clothes
ISBN 0 7496 6151 8*
ISBN 0 7496 6163 1

The Pied Piper of Hamelin
ISBN 0 7496 6152 6*
ISBN 0 7496 6164 X

Hansel and Gretel
ISBN 0 7496 6150 X*
ISBN 0 7496 6162 3

The Sleeping Beauty
ISBN 0 7496 6148 8*
ISBN 0 7496 6160 7

Rumpelstiltskin
ISBN 0 7496 6153 4*
ISBN 0 7496 6165 8

The Ugly Duckling
ISBN 0 7496 6154 2*
ISBN 0 7496 6166 6

Puss in Boots
ISBN 0 7496 6155 0*
ISBN 0 7496 6167 4

The Frog Prince
ISBN 0 7496 6156 9*
ISBN 0 7496 6168 2

The Princess and the Pea
ISBN 0 7496 6157 7*
ISBN 0 7496 6169 0

Dick Whittington
ISBN 0 7496 6158 5*
ISBN 0 7496 6170 4

* hardback